# A Mother for Choco

## Keiko Kasza

PUFFIN BOOKS

To Bela and Ange
and to all the children who have
found their own Mrs. Bear

PUFFIN BOOKS
Published by the Penguin Group
Penguin Putnam Books for Young Readers, 345 Hudson Street, New York, New York 10014, U.S.A.
Penguin Books Ltd, 27 Wrights Lane, London W8 5TZ, England
Penguin Books Australia Ltd, Ringwood, Victoria, Australia
Penguin Books Canada Ltd, 10 Alcorn Avenue, Toronto, Ontario, Canada M4V 3B2
Penguin Books (N.Z.) Ltd, 182-190 Wairau Road, Auckland 10, New Zealand

Penguin Books Ltd, Registered Offices: Harmondsworth, Middlesex, England

Originally published in a different form in Japan by Saera Shobo (Librarie Çà et Là), copyright © 1982 Keiko Kasza
First published in the United States of America by G. P. Putnam's Sons, 1992
Published by PaperStar, a division of the Putnam & Grosset Group, 1996
Published by Puffin Books, a member of Penguin Putnam Books for Young Readers, 1999

3  5  7  9  10  8  6  4

LIBRARY OF CONGRESS CATALOGING-IN-PUBLICATION DATA:
A mother for Choco/Keiko Kasza.  p.  cm.
Summary: A lonely little bird named Choco goes in search of a mother.
[1. Mothers—Fiction. 2. Love—Fiction 3. Birds—Fiction.]  I. Title.
PZ7.K15645Mo 1992 [E]—dc20 91-12361 CIP AC
ISBN 0-698-11364-0

Printed in the U.S.A.

$C$hoco was a little bird, who lived all alone. He wished he had a mother, but who could his mother be? One day he set off to find her.

First Choco met Mrs. Giraffe.

"Oh, Mrs. Giraffe!" he cried. "You are yellow just like me! Are you my mother?"

"I'm sorry," sighed Mrs. Giraffe. "But I don't have wings like you."

Next Choco met Mrs. Penguin.

"Oh, Mrs. Penguin!" he cried. "You have wings just like me! Are you my mother?"

"I'm sorry," sighed Mrs. Penguin. "But I don't have big, round cheeks like you."

Then Choco met Mrs. Walrus.

"Oh, Mrs. Walrus!" he cried. "You have big, round cheeks just like me. Are you my mother?"

"Now look," grumped Mrs. Walrus. "I don't have striped feet like you, so don't bother me!"

No matter where Choco searched, he couldn't find a mother who looked just like him.

When Choco saw Mrs. Bear picking
apples, he knew she couldn't be his
mother. Mrs. Bear didn't look like him
at all.

Choco was so sad he started to cry. "Mommy, mommy! I need a mommy!"

Mrs. Bear came running to see what was the matter. As she listened to Choco's story, she sighed. "Oh, dear. If you had a mommy, what would she do?"

"Oh, I'm sure she would hold me," sobbed Choco.

"Like this?" asked Mrs. Bear. And she held Choco very tight.

"Yes . . . and I'm sure she would kiss me, too!" said Choco.

"Like this?" asked Mrs. Bear. And she lifted Choco and gave him a big kiss.

"Yes, and I'm sure she would sing and dance with me to cheer me up," said Choco.

"Like this?" asked Mrs. Bear. And they sang and danced together.

When they stopped to rest, Mrs. Bear turned to Choco and said, "Choco, maybe I could be your mother."

"*You?*" Choco cried.

"But you aren't yellow. And you don't have wings, or big, round cheeks, or striped feet like me!"

"My goodness!" said Mrs. Bear. "That would make me look very funny!" Choco thought it was funny, too.

"Well," said Mrs. Bear, "my other children are waiting for me at home. Why don't you join us for apple pie, Choco?"

Apple pie sounded wonderful to Choco, so off they went.

When they arrived, Mrs. Bear's other children rushed out to greet her.

"Choco," said Mrs. Bear. "Meet Hippy, Ally, and Piggy. I am their mother, too!"

The sweet smell of apple pie and the sound
of laughter soon filled Mrs. Bear's home.

After their delicious treat, Mrs. Bear gave all her children a big, warm bear hug.

And Choco was very happy that his new mommy looked just the way she did.